Listen closely.

No, really closely.

Christmas almost didn't happen one year!

Don't shake your head — something might come loose in your brain.

Don't giggle.

This isn't funny. (Well, **sometimes** it is.)

Anyway, here's what happened.

And how I got to be

santaKid.

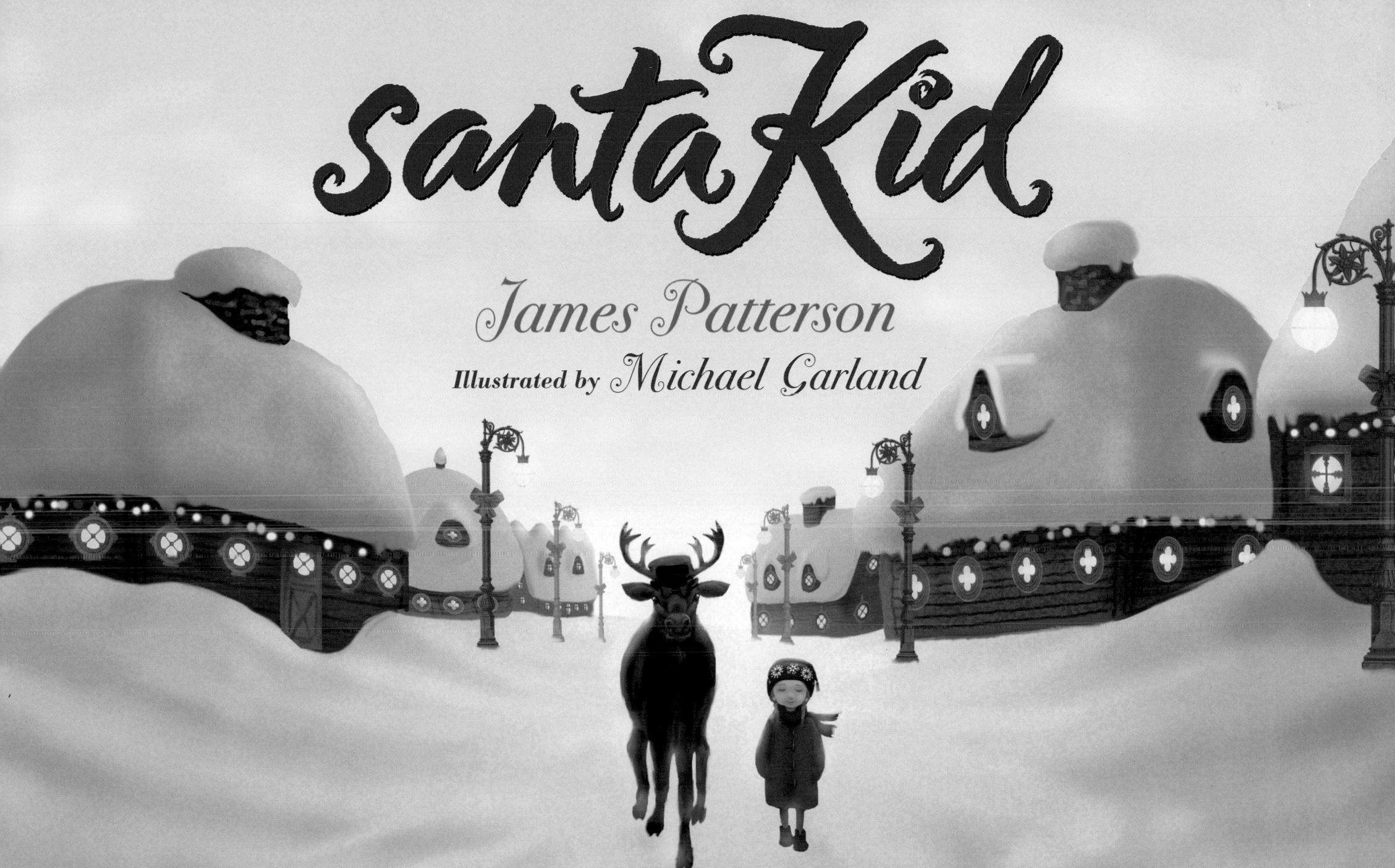

santaKid

James Patterson

Illustrated by Michael Garland

headline

Hi! My name is Chrissie
and I live at the North Pole.
Pretty cool, huh?
Certainly is, 'cause every day I get to go to Santa's Toy Workshop
and play with Santa's reindeer and the Christmas doves and the Christmas mice
and Santa's Elves — like Ooff, who's six foot eleven (tall for an Elf).
Know why I get to live at the North Pole?
Because my daddy and mummy are Mr and Mrs Santa Claus!
I'm Santa's little girl.

All those who want to live at the North Pole, shout:

"I WANT TO LIVE AT THE NORTH POLE!"

If you came to the North Pole, you'd get some real surprises. Like this:

all year long, except at Christmastime . . .

Santa has *no* beard.

No jolly mounds of fat

(not good for the heart).

But at Christmastime, Santa grows a beard.

And Mummy Claus bleaches it white

and puts stuffing in Santa's red suit.

Other than that, Santa is like most other dads —

he loves me more than anything in the world.

Santa taught me lots of cool things,

but there was *a whole lot* I didn't understand about Christmas.

Like how can Santa remember where every single kid lives

to deliver the right presents?

And how does he fit all the presents on one sleigh?

And how come the reindeer can fly on Christmas Eve?

My dad, Santa Claus, would just smile and say,

"Chrissie, you have to believe."

"Believe in *what*?" I asked, my eyes open wide.

"You have to believe in something bigger than yourself."

I laughed. "*Everything's* bigger than me!" I said.

"That's it!" Santa clapped. "Now never forget it."

The job that Santa and Mummy Claus gave me

was to feed the reindeer — Donner, Blitzen, and gang.

And to hang out with my best reindeer friend, Rhymer —

who wears a funky top hat and was born on the same day as me.

One morning, Rhymer and I heard a roar in the skies.

We looked up and saw an aeroplane landing at Reindeer Field.

The plane had writing all over it that said:

EXMAS EXPRESS, EXMAS EXPRESS.

"Must be somebody big in *Biz-ness*," rhymed Rhymer.

"Let's go see *Who-it-is-ness*."

We didn't know it, but everything was about to change.

The Big Boss of the Exmas Express company

was named Vernon Ransom, and he was not nice. Definitely not nice.

That morning, Vernon marched into Santa's office

at the Toy Workshop — *like he owned it.*

"WE'RE HERE TO BUY THE NORTH POLE," he shouted,

because Vernon Ransom always shouted everything.

"ACTUALLY, WE'RE HERE TO BUY CHRISTMAS."

Santa couldn't believe it.

"Oh, Christmas isn't for sale," he said with a *ho-ho-ho!*

Then Vernon Ransom laughed, too. A very loud, very mean laugh.

"YOU'D BETTER BELIEVE THIS!" he told Santa. "EVERYTHING'S FOR SALE."

Suddenly the news was on every TV,

in the newspapers, even on Nickelodeon.

NORTH POLE BOUGHT BY EXMAS EXPRESS!
CHRISTMAS TO BE CALLED EXMAS!
SANTA HAS A NEW BOSS!

All my friends at the North Pole were in a bit of a state.

But especially Santa, who just couldn't believe that Christmas had been bought.

But trust me, I saw it with my own eyes.

Everything at the North Pole seemed to change overnight.

The Christmas doves wouldn't fly or sing.

Ooff and the other Elves stopped making toys.

The Exmas Express company families

began to arrive in their shiny black cars.

Exmas Express was at the North Pole to run everything.

And everybody.

And every thought.

At all times of the day and night.

Now, when I went to the Toy Workshop, everybody looked so glum and gloomy.

Exmas Express was making new kinds of toys.

Toys like:

Weird Wally Warmunga the Warrior.

Princess PeePee and PooPoo.

Doggie DooDoo.

And everybody's least favourite,

the 315th Day Toy.

Which, on the 315th day of the year, every year . . .

fell apart!!!

"Not nice," Ooff, the six-foot-eleven-inch Elf said to me.

"Just not very nice at all."

It was the worst thing Ooff had ever said in his long, tall life.

I almost didn't want to go to the Toy Workshop.

Vernon Ransom was a large, angry person whose face was almost as red as Santa's suit.

"LET ME *EXPRESS* MYSELF CLEARLY," yelled Vernon.

"WE'RE WAY BEHIND SCHEDULE.
RIGHT NOW, ONLY TWENTY-ONE PERCENT OF CHILDREN
WILL GET TOYS FOR EXMAS!"

I groaned in disbelief.

"OUR *GOAL*," said Vernon, "IS FIFTY PERCENT!
FIVE OUT OF TEN CHILDREN WILL GET PRESENTS THIS EXMAS!"

I couldn't believe my ears.

I ran to tell Santa and get his help.

Santa had stopped going to the Toy Workshop.

Then he stopped going out of the house.

Finally he stopped getting out of bed.

He began to put on a lot of weight.

And grew a long, white beard.

Santa started looking like Santa.

And not in a good way.

I burst into Santa's bedroom and told him

the terrible news from the Toy Workshop.

"I guess I don't believe in Christmas any more," he said.

It was the saddest thing I'd ever heard.

"Well, *I* believe," I whispered.

"I'll always believe in Christmas."

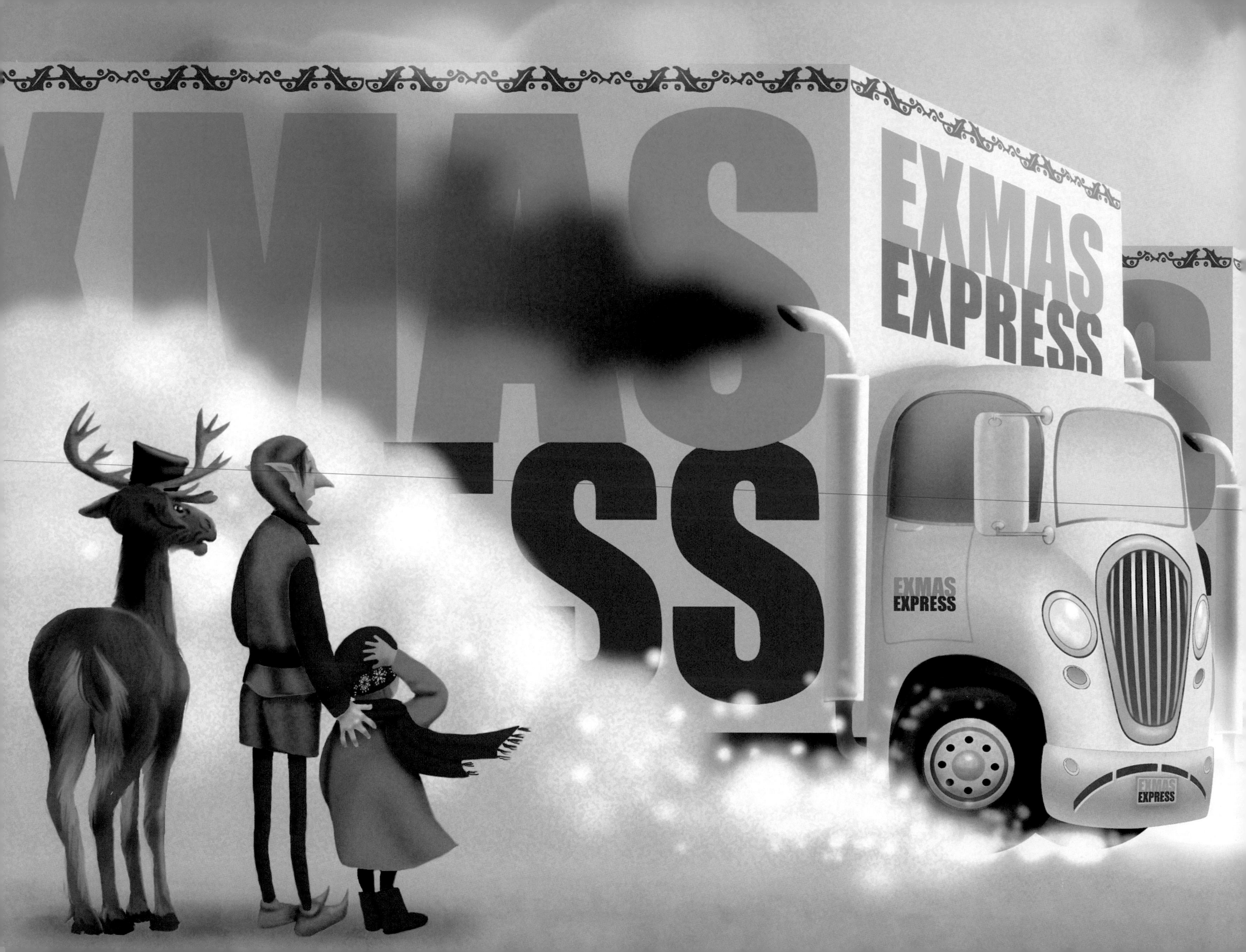
EXMAS
EXPRESS
EXMAS
EXPRESS
EXMAS
EXPRESS

The next day, spirits at the North Pole

sank lower than a reindeer's bum.

Exmas carols began to fill the air.

Exmas cards were being written, with *Exmas* rhymes.

Nobody laughed or smiled at the Toy Workshop.

And Santa didn't seem to care. He just stayed in bed.

And ate his weight in cream cakes.

Meanwhile, the new Exmas Express trucks arrived.

Thousands of them — white as snow, with bright red trim —

to replace Santa's beautiful sleigh and the reindeer, too.

Christmas was going to be ruined this year.

And maybe for ever,

which is a long time for something to be ruined.

So I decided to do something.

You have to believe, I reminded myself, *in something bigger than yourself.*

I rode Rhymer the Reindeer over to Vernon Ransom's house.

Vernon answered the door.

I made myself as brave as can be, and I said,

"Hi, I'm Chrissie!"

"SO WHAT?" shouted Vernon Ransom.

I took a deep breath and kept talking.

"You can't just buy Christmas! You can't buy the North Pole!

Exmas Express is ruining everything that's good and beautiful."

"YOU'RE WASTING MY TIME, AND TIME IS MONEY," Vernon shouted.

Then he said the worst thing of all.

The worst thing any kid could hear.

"GO AWAY. A KID HAS NOTHING GOOD TO SAY."

In a wink, in a blink, it was Christmas Eve.

The magic night was here.

But where was the magic?

Exmas Express trucks stuttered and sputtered.

Some were stuck in snow drifts up to their ugly logos.

The Christmas presents weren't being delivered.

Not five out of ten!

Not one out of ten!

Vernon Ransom screamed at the Elves, "THIS IS YOUR FAULT — IT'S NONE OF MY DOING.
I'LL HAVE YOUR POINTY-EARED HEADS IN THE MORNING."

I ran home to Santa as fast as I could. I brought everybody with me —

Mummy Claus, the reindeer, and the Elves.

"You have to save Christmas!" I begged Santa.

But my dad just looked at me.

"Do you believe, Chrissie, . . . in something bigger than yourself?"

There were tears in my eyes, and I could barely find my voice.

"Yes, I believe. I've always believed."

Then Santa smiled. "I'm too heavy for the sleigh," he said.

"But if you believe, you can save Christmas yourself."

Well, I'll tell you, I had the whole North Pole buzzing.

The Elves were smiling, and so were the reindeer, and even the Christmas mice.

We hauled out Santa's sleigh and all the "good" toys.

No Princess PeePee and PooPoo, no Doggie DooDoo.

Everybody pitched in. Everybody believed in the magic.

But did I? Did I believe enough?

How could I possibly know the address of every single kid?

How could all these toys fit into the sleigh?

Then Vernon Ransom ran towards me.

"KID, THIS WON'T FLY!" he yelled.

"SANTA'S SLEIGH WON'T WORK WITHOUT SANTA!"

I looked him in the eye, and here's what I said:

"Kids are small, but kids are smart.

Kids are smart enough to understand the magic of Christmas."

And then the most amazing thing — THE MAGIC HAPPENED —

the reindeer flew, the sleigh full of toys took off, and so did I.

I believed in Christmas in a way I never had before.

I believed in how special and holy it was.

I believed that I would know every address of every kid in every country.

I believed that Rhymer and the other reindeer could fly all night and never get tired.

And then, when I was flying past a falling star,

a little boy leaned from his bedroom window and called out,

"Where's Santa? He always comes!"

But then he spotted a sleigh in the sky.

And reindeer! And — something even more incredible!

A kid was driving Santa's sleigh!

Could it be?

A kid just like him — little hands, arms, legs, teeth, and a big smile?

And then the little boy made it official.

"It's santaKid!" he shouted up to my sleigh. "I see santaKid!"

Believe me, I was having the night of my life.

The night of any kid's life.

Delivering Christmas presents to everybody everywhere.

I remembered every single kid, and where they lived.

And that means — *I came to your house, too!*

And at the end of the long, long night,

after I stopped at every kid's house, every tent, every hut, and every block of flats,

I made one last stop . . . at Vernon Ransom's house.

Vernon's kids were crying and so was Vernon's wife.

And so was Vernon —

because he'd never *not* got his Christmas presents.

I gave everybody their gifts, then I shook Vernon's hand.

"NO HARD FEELINGS, KID!" he yelled.

"No hard feelings," I said, "But you and your friends and your broken-down trucks

and your shiny black cars have to get out of the North Pole by New Year's Day."

And that's what happened.

That night, Christmas night, I had the most scrumpilicious dinner ever

with my family and all my friends.

And my dad finally asked,

"Chrissie, did you really deliver all those presents to all those kids?"

And I had to tell him the truth.

"Well, I didn't exactly deliver the presents in the usual way."

There was quiet in the room.

"I talked to every kid, and do you know what I told them?

I told them Christmas isn't about getting presents.

I told the kids that Christmas is about something much, much bigger than presents. Christmas is about believing!"

"Wow!" said my dad, and everybody around our table joined in. "That's what happened? That's great!"

I started to laugh and then I winked at Santa and Mummy Claus.

"Yeah — and then I gave everybody their presents!"

For Jack and Susie
—J. P.

To my Uncle Billy
—M. G.

First Published in Great Britain in 2004
by HEADLINE BOOK PUBLISHING

10 9 8 7 6 5 4 3 2 1

Cataloguing in Publication Data is available from the British Library

ISBN 0 7553 2204 5
The illustrations for this book were created digitally.

Printed and bound in Italy by Canale C. S. p. A

HEADLINE BOOK PUBLISHING
A division of Hodder Headline
338 Euston Road
London NW1 3BH

www.headline.co.uk
www.hodderheadline.com

Believe!

From santaKid
and all your friends
at the North Pole
who love you!

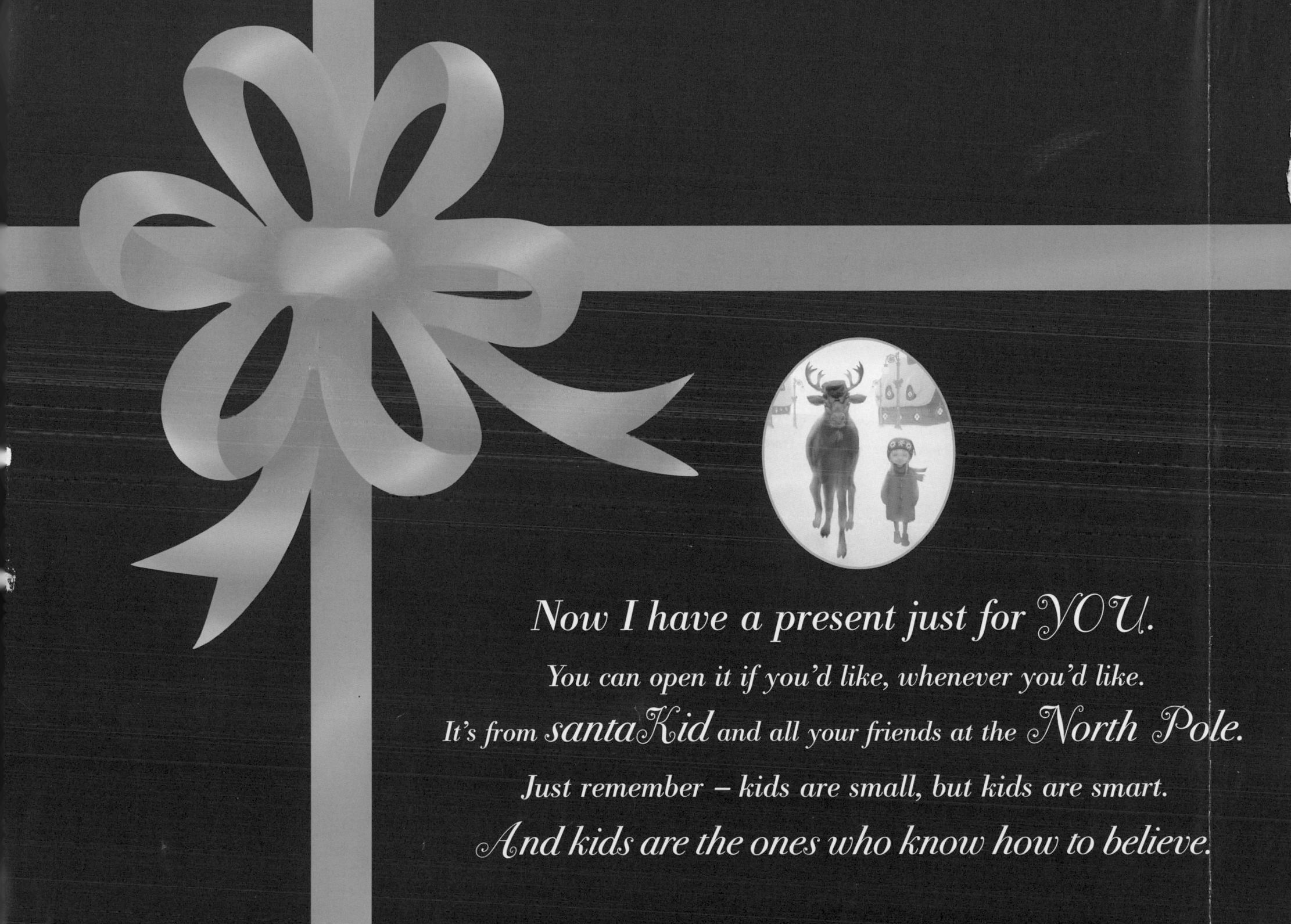

Now I have a present just for *YOU*.

You can open it if you'd like, whenever you'd like.

It's from *santaKid* and all your friends at the *North Pole*.

Just remember — kids are small, but kids are smart.

And kids are the ones who know how to believe.